To all the children from
the multi-schools council
for all their hard work.

We may all be different but
we have the same smile

A 'JAJAJA' BOOK

First published in Great Britain in 2018 by JaJaJa Books

Text copyright © 2018 Genevieve Yusuf
Illustration copyright © 2018 Shermain Philip

Design by Karen Clark

The author's and the illustrator's moral rights have been asserted.

ISBN 978-0-9569411-8-3

Printed in Great Britain

www.jajaja-books.com

Sam woke up with a cloud on her head,

A cloud on her head as she stepped out of bed.

She put on her clothes, not feeling quite right,
But stepped out the door and the sun seemed too bright.

"Hey there, dear Sammy," said Spider that day.

(They'd been friends forever, and friends they would stay.)

Spider could listen to Sam all day long,

He knew how it felt if a day just went wrong.

"I'm not looking forward to school," stated Sam.

"C'moooooon," said Spider, "you know that you can."

"You've had days like this before, my dear friend.

Let's give it a go, now let's start again."

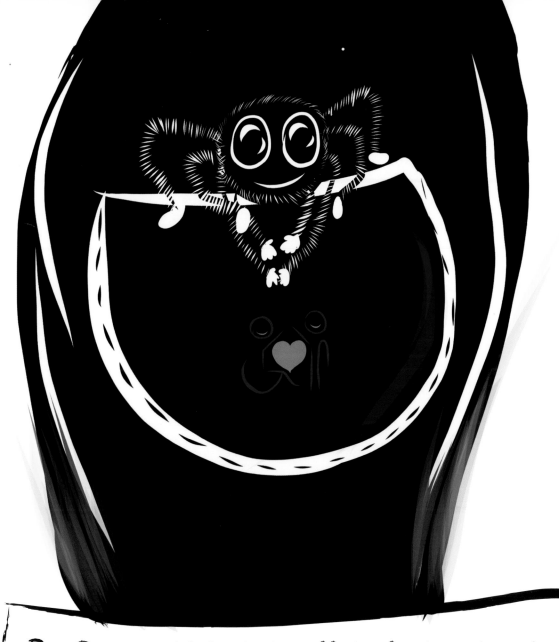

But Sam couldn't shake off the feeling that day.

Spider climbed into her pocket to stay.

School seemed so noisy, the room seemed too bright,
Everyone's voice made Sam feel all tight...

...in her tummy and made her head feel very strange,

The work was too hard and words jumped on the page.

Sam tried to shout and make herself heard,
She kicked at her chair, she pushed and she squirmed.

She got told to go to a place to calm down,
And Spider hopped out - Sam's face had a frown.

"Oh Sam, my dear girl, please do not be sad.

You're not misbehaving, you're not being bad.

Remember how brilliant you can be with art,

With maths and with sport - and that's just the start."

"Don't worry about others, that stare or that laugh,
Remember what people say when I'm in the bath."

"They scream and they shout, they're frightened of me.

They misunderstand and don't want to see,

I'm kind and I'm helpful, I'll work all day long.

I make massive webs which are pretty and strong."

"We all have bad days my Sammy, you know."

"But some can be good, so please don't feel low."

"You're smart and you're funny and people will see,

They just need some patience, and that is the key,

To knowing, my Sammy, so chin up, my girl –

You're the best friend a spider could have in the world."

THE END

We may all be different but
we have the same smile

The multi-schools council

The multi-schools council is committed to breaking down perceptions about children with disabilities, special educational needs and social, emotional and mental health difficulties. By creating more awareness about our differences, we hope that society will come to a better understanding of those differences and will be more accepting of them.

The idea for this book came from the children – and that underpins the whole ethos of the 'pupil voice' of our council.

Any school can join the multi-schools council by emailing
kierran.pearce@marketfield.essex.sch.uk

If we work together we will break down perceptions.

After every multi-schools meeting or event, my child comes home and teaches us so much about autism and lots of different needs. He is so enthusiastic about breaking down barriers for all types of people.

The multi-schools council gives children who don't always have a voice the chance to be heard.

When our children visited the special school for the first time, they were amazed by what they saw. Giving all types of children the chance to see different schools is a great way of breaking down perceptions.

JaJaJa Books

To find more titles by JaJaJa Books go to

www.jajaja-books.com